Bob the Builder™

Wendy's Big Match

One bright sunny morning, Bob was reading in the yard.

"What's that?" Dizzy asked excitedly.

"It's a flower catalogue," Bob replied. "I'm ordering some flowers because I've entered us in the Brightest Building Yard Competition."

"But the yard's a mess!" cried Muck.

Bob nodded. "We're going to have a big tidy up before the judges arrive!"

"When are they coming?" asked Roley.

"At five o'clock," replied Bob.

"You'd better get started then," called Wendy, as she walked into the yard. "Muck can help you, Bob. The rest of the machines can come with me – we've got to get the football pitch ready today."

As Wendy jumped aboard Scoop, Bob popped Dizzy's football on top of her mixer.

"Have fun!" he called after them.

"**Can we build it?**" yelled Wendy, as they roared out of the yard.

"**Yes, we can!**" cried the machines.

When Wendy and the machines got to the football field, Dizzy started to run around after her ball.

"Brilliant! A proper pitch right here!" she squealed as she booted the football.

"Mind out, Dizzy," rumbled Roley. "I need to get this grass as flat as I can. If I leave any bumps, the ball will bounce all over the place."

Scoop unloaded the white paint and Wendy filled up the line-marking machine.

"What a team!" said Wendy proudly.

Over at the yard, Bob started tidying up, while Muck went to pick up the plants and flowers.

"Miaow!" grumbled Pilchard, as the dust flew up her nose.

"Sorry Pilchard, but it's going to be difficult getting this yard cleaned up in time," said Bob.

Back at the football field, Wendy was busy marking out a goal line. Scoop was unloading the timber for the goal posts and Roley was flattening the ground. But Dizzy was bored and wanted to play football.

Spud popped up from behind a bush and giggled, "Heh, heh, heh! I'll play!"

Dizzy passed the ball to Spud, who gave it a huge **Kick!**
It flew high into the sky, then dropped slowly down.

"Oh, no!" squeaked Dizzy. "It's going to land on Wendy!"

Wendy looked up and saw it heading straight for her. Dragging the line-marking machine she ducked sideways, and the ball just missed her.

"Where did that come from?" she gasped.

"Er, Wendy," gulped Scoop. "Look what you've done."

Wendy gazed in horror at the wiggly line she'd made on the pitch.

Spud tried to sneak away. "Time to go," he muttered.

"Spud! Did you just kick that ball?" asked Wendy sternly.

Spud nodded. "Sorry, Wendy. I didn't mean to mess up your line. I was just showing Dizzy a few football tricks."

Wendy glared at Spud. "Well, now you can fetch a bucket and brush, and show Dizzy a few cleaning-up tricks!" she told him.

"Spud's on the job, Bob… I mean, Wendy. Heh, heh, heh!" giggled the naughty scarecrow.

Back at the yard, Bob was very busy.

"**Miaow!**" grumbled Pilchard as Bob stepped over her.

"Oh, Pilchard!" cried Bob. "Find somewhere else to sleep!"

Pilchard stalked off in a big sulk. She found a warm, sunny spot on top of the pile of rubbish that Bob had just swept up! She curled up and was soon snoozing.

Muck came roaring back into the yard with his front dumper full of plants and flowers.

"Here I am, Bob!" cried Muck.

"Well done, Muck," said Bob. "Let's get those plants unloaded. Then we can start clearing away that pile of rubbish."

While Bob arranged his flowerpots, Muck busily scooped up all the building rubbish in his back dumper. He had no idea that Pilchard was fast asleep on the rubbish heap.

"**Mi-aa-oo-w!**" she howled crossly.

Bob turned around when he heard Pilchard's loud cries.

"Oh, no! Muck, **STOP!**" he yelled, as Muck thundered out of the yard with Pilchard wailing on top of his loaded dumper!

Muck slammed on his brakes and whizzed sharply around, sending rubbish flying all over the yard.

"What's the prob, Bob?"

"You've scooped up Pilchard with the rubbish!" cried Bob.

"**Miaow!**" yelped Pilchard, as she leapt off Muck and jumped straight into Bob's arms.

"Sorry," gulped Muck. "I didn't realise you were up there, Pilchard."

As Bob put up his hanging baskets, Bird settled comfortably on one of the new flowerpots. "**Tweet!**" he chirruped happily.

"Bird! I know my pots make a lovely nest but you're flattening my flowers," grumbled Bob.

Bird hooted and flew off, but a few minutes later Bob found him perched on top of the other plant pot. Bob sighed heavily. "You're squashing **those** flowers too, Bird. I don't think I'll **ever** have the yard clean and tidy by five o'clock!"

Wendy was making good progress on the football pitch. Lofty had lifted the goal posts into position. Roley had flattened the pitch perfectly. Scoop had helped Wendy to build the grandstand. Spud had even cleaned up the wiggly white line.

"Oh, Wendy," squeaked Dizzy. "Please can we play a game of football?"

"I think we've got time," said Wendy checking her watch. "We're not due back at the yard until five o'clock."

"**Yippeee!**" shrieked Dizzy as she raced down the field after the ball.

22

Wendy blew her whistle to start the big match. Dizzy kicked off. And when Lofty got the ball, Dizzy nipped in and sent it up the field to Spud. Spud trapped the ball and headed it over to Wendy. **Wheee!** Wendy dribbled the ball towards the open goalmouth and **Wham!** She booted it in.

Goal!!!

"What a goal!" yelled Dizzy. "Hooray for Wendy!"

"**Hurray!**" they all cheered.

"Oh, that was fun!" gasped Wendy. "But we must get back to the yard," she said. "It's nearly five o'clock.

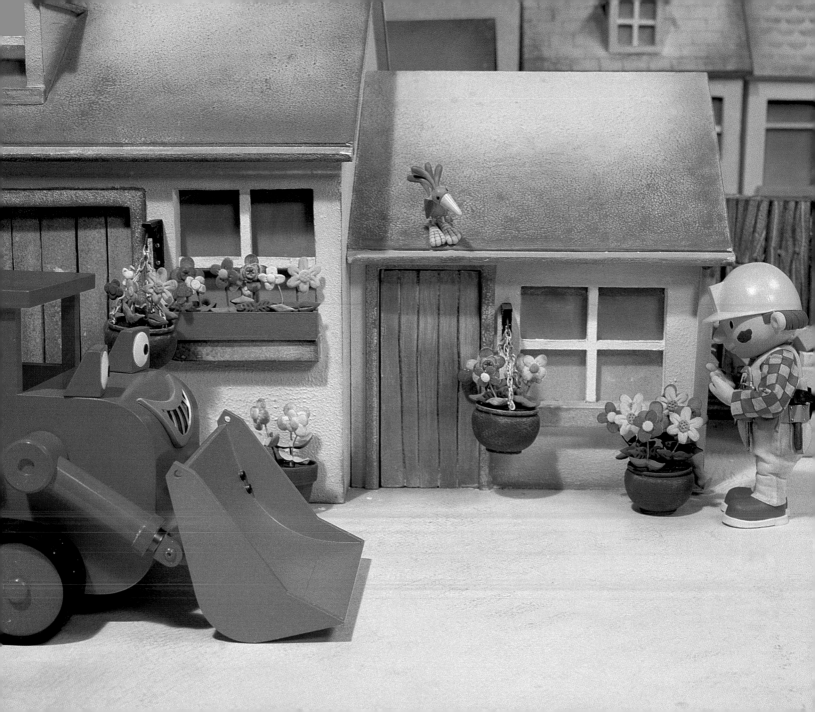

The yard was finished in time, too. It looked bright and clean and very tidy, but Bob's face and overalls were covered in dirt!

"I'd better go and smarten myself up before the judges arrive," he said to Muck.

Suddenly they heard a car draw up outside the yard.

"I think we've got visitors," said Muck.

"Oh, no!" gasped Bob. "The judges are early!"

When Wendy and the machines arrived back at the yard, they were amazed at how smart and tidy it looked.

"It's really, really pretty!" squeaked Dizzy.

"Er, it looks lovely, Bob… I think," mumbled Lofty.

"Cool!" rumbled Roley.

"You've done a great job, Bob," said Wendy.

Suddenly she spotted Bird snuggled down in one of the flowerpots by the office door. "Bird! Get out of there before the judges arrive!" she cried.

"It's too late for that," said Bob. "The judges came early. They've already been and gone."

"Really?" said Wendy. "What did they say?"

"Yeah, tell us Bob," begged Dizzy.

"What happened, Bob?" asked Scoop. Bob just smiled.

"Tell me what the judges said," Dizzy squeaked excitedly. "Muck, please tell me!"

Muck went very red in the face and turned to Bob. "You tell them!" he cried.

"We **won!**" yelled Bob as he held up the award. "Our yard won first prize in the Brightest Building Yard Competition!"

"Yippee!"

"Whoo-hoo!" cheered the machines.

"Oh, Bob, that's wonderful," cried Wendy. "Well done!"

"The yard looks really clean, Bob," giggled Dizzy, "but you're all mucky and dirty."

Wendy smiled and took out her hanky to wipe some smudgy marks off Bob's face.

"Lucky for you it wasn't the Brightest Builder Competition," she teased.

"You're right there, Wendy!" laughed Bob.

THE END!